LEE

Reluctantly, I'm sitting in front of the cruel, hairdresser's mirror with harsh, bright, spot lights fixed on my 'greys' and laughter-lines (*who am I kidding at 45?, laughter lines indeed, why I've got 20 years behind me, using sunbeds and taking last minute getaways to Tenerife...My skin now looks like the back end of Nelly the elephant!*)

The client next to me, is recalling her antics of the previous night, whereby she'd 'hooked-up with Mike from Tinder' who had turned out to be not quite as virile as she had been led to believe previously by his saucy-sexting and to her dismay, he'd run-out of little blue pills that could 'help things along a bit'.......and as he explained, in great detail, whilst both of them lay staring somberly at the ceiling, later that night, 'he'd never had this much difficulty before and she really wasn't much of a helping hand.' Therefore, she had to conclude that, the problem obviously laid squarely with her, ''poor cow!'' and leaving no doubt that she'd have 'Old-Faithful' out from the bedside cabinet once again this evening, after a warm bath and a couple of glasses of Chardonnay! 'Old Faithful would never let her down although the batteries had once or twice after extended....cough, cough...(she lowered her voice)...play.'

 I had acknowledged earlier in the week that a trip to the hairdresser's was looming, especially as I'd gotten so lucky, that a blackberry eating starling had selected to bestow his blessings upon me and ejected a massive, purple, crap-splat upon my head.

 I'd put it off for a few weeks as my old friend, stylist and confidant Daphne had taken her leave and took her dexterous fingers off to live in sunnier-climes with her first ever, Summer-love Philippe. Daphne had creased, ample, bronzed boobs and a long, gold chain that comfortably nestled between them. A curly, blond 'cougar' with straight, bleached teeth. She'd tracked Philippe down on the internet and subsequently had left her husband, Arthur, within 3 months of being reacquainted with 'Pip!'

 I'll tell you more about her another day....God, I miss that gal!

Anyway back to me, sitting in the electric chair, oops hairdresser's chair!

I had booked with Leigh, she had an available 2.30 appointment.

Leigh turned out to be Lee, a rather flamboyant chap in a Jazzy shirt and jaunty cap worn to one side .He had 4 buttons undone revealing a silky smooth, tanned

chest. He smelt gorgeous,
'And what would Madam like today?' he enquired of me beginning to lift my long unkempt hair above my head as if it was about to catch fire at any moment....

(At exactly what age is 'too old for long hair, these days? Should it have already gone in my 30's ? I guess the 'Kate Bush look' was wearing a bit thin nowadays although she had recently sold out the Royal Albert Hall and still looked 'Absolutely Fabulous Darling!' fluttering about the stage seeking Heathcliff in an unconsoleable manner.) I cleared my throat,

'Oh, just a bit of a tidy-up really,' I said, sinking a little further down into my chair. What I really wanted to say was, 'Please, please, please make me beautiful again!' I took a crumpled photo out of my pocket to show Lee (I'd been carrying it around with me for 'some time now') of a woman less than half my age with the hair of an angel. A wry smile flickered at the corners of his lips and then he simply said to me,

 'Oh, Madam wants to look like a pre 'Toxic', Britney Spears'? …..yes, well, of course, we do keep a time-machine out the back for such occasions, oh look, here comes Dr Who now!'

#How bloody rude!.

I let his mean spirited remark 'go' (well, at my age, I didn't want to cause a scene did I?) quite frankly, looking at myself, at such close quarters, he wasn't wrong!

It was actually, surprisingly, easy to forgive this young man who wore his scissors and combs slung around his hips in a black, leather holster (very sexy). I could imagine him as a cowboy out-west, strutting into some dusty, American town…… growling out the corner of his mouth….

'I've come for my 2.30 appointment......where the hell is she?' ... the ladies would giggle nervously from behind their 'Hello and Cosmo' magazines.........he sure was purdy :) but for the next 40 minutes, Deputy Sheriff Lee was all mine.

I'd already had my hair washed by Frieda. Who invents those awfully uncomfortable sinks by the way, especially the reverse ones, where you face upwards, gazing at the swirly pattern of the artexed ceiling, whilst the jet of water shoots its way down your back, finally being absorbed by your cotton knickers, (it's just too bad for you, if you're wearing undies that are anything less substantial than a sturdy pair from M&S,) and all the time, you're trying to keep a lame conversation ongoing about how long your last spray tan lasted, was it 3 or 4 days? (Snore,) and Frieda asks,

'Is the water too hot for you?'...to which the rest of the salon hears my reply,

'Ahhhhhhhh,' I think she's just scolded my flipping nipps with the wayward jet spray! (you know I'm being polite there, don't you:) ... it's like I'm on a frigging water ride at Alton Tower's but a damn sight less L.M.P. (that's 'Laughing My Pants off,' ....O.M.G! ...'Oh My God!' it doesn't mean that at all, I just double-checked the abbreviation in the Urban Dictionary and you might wish to enlighten yourself too.

Reverse sinks come from the same, 'madhouse of invention,' as TEAPOTS THAT DON'T POUR STRAIGHT! For flip-sake...(polite once more,) don't get me started on those. How many times have you had to lift your teacup or mug (we're not posh 'ere, you know,) whilst a soggy, paper napkin clings on to the bottom of it like Leonardo Dicaprio clung to that piece of driftwood in the mighty film Titanic....?

And there WOULD have been room for him to get on that floating plank if damn Kate

Winslet had shifted her butt over a bit! Really, how selfish can you get!

And we've all got our own opinion's about that, haven't we?

Grrrrr…..

ARTHUR

Arthur's new neighbour casually said hello across the privet and politely asked how his wife was as he hadn't seen her for a goodly while.

'Oh, I buried her in the back garden last weekend,' Arthur replied rudely turning his back, yet smiling to himself that the old jokes were always the best, nosey bloody neighbours he thought. It was common knowledge that Daphne had left him for a younger man about a month ago now.

Why, when they had moved in about 2 months back now, neither one of them could be bothered to visit the other to introduce themselves properly and now it had reached that uneasy stage when it was too awkward to ask each other's name. Not that Arthur really cared, he didn't like them anyway. There was no reason for this, however the brand new Ford Focus on next door's forecourt did upset him, as front gardens should be preserved for standard roses and evergreens, Arthur cleared his throat in an unpleasant fashion. The funny thing about this was that he had been digging over the compost heap towards the end of the back-garden, under the twisted apple tree and had installed some new decking too. A great spot to 'rest,' he'd chuckled darkly and placed an old wooden bench there.

He couldn't understand why Daphne had left him so abruptly, he was telling an old friend. She was a fantastic home-maker and loved his wicked sense of humour. There was that hilarious time just before she went, that the 'Mrs' had stepped naked from the ensuite, into the bedroom, and Arthur had exclaimed as quick as lightning,

'I don't know what you're wearing but it needs a bloody good iron!'......absolute classic he laughed out loud before turning back to the mirror to drag the last hair out from the top of his large moonscape nose with some rusty tweezers. ha ha ha ha ha.

That night, Josh and Tilly lay in bed feeling sorry for their next door neighbour, despite his earlier bad manners. They could hear him below. They thought mistakenly that he was calling sadly out to his missing wife into the cold night sky from his back doorstep.

'Margaret, Margaret where are you, come back sweetheart, please come back.'

But Arthur was shouting to Maggie, his little dog that was too busy digging around the old compost area by the apple tree, to take any notice of her master.

Arthur quipped to himself the next day when he discovered the hole in the garden that she had dug

'Like a dog with a bone,' ...ha ha ha ha ha, (he did enjoy his own jokes.)

He settled the earth back down with his spade and added some decorative stones.

 'No one would ever know now, it's as good as new,' he sniffed loudly and scratched his faithful dog on her head, who was once again by his side.

FRIEDA

Frieda had been training under Daphne's supervision for about a year before she had unexpectedly left the salon but now she was *under* Lee. He had many 'female friends,' and Frieda never knew for sure who was his favourite of the month but he assured her that she was his very own little special lady who he could never do without, especially in the staff's kitchen where he would often nuzzle her neck and squeeze her bum as he reached across for the tints or spare hair-straighteners. Frieda had just turned 18 and 'so no harm done,' Lee reasoned with himself, 'she's a big girl now,'....On her special Birthday, Lee had accidentally left her gift and card at home he lied, what he'd actually done was left them on the shelf at the gift shop. He leered at her standing by the reception desk and felt a familiar twinge. Lee was 10 years older than her, married to Lyndsay, a stylist who was on extended maternity leave from the 'Curl-up n Dye,' (the salon's rather odd name) with their second child. Lee breathed deeply, adjusted himself and went to find his next blow dry.

Frieda dreaded the day that Lyndsay would return to work as she was totally in love and knew that it was only a matter of time before Lee would leave his wife and kids to be with her. They would live in a camper-van if they had to (that was his dream, apparently). He just needed a bit more time, the baby had been a mistake and he'd only had sex with his wife because he'd argued with Frieda that day and he thought things were over between them......he's so, so sorry.

Actually, Lee couldn't keep his hands off his wife's ballooning, engorged body, she was his elixir. It was like the old days of being with his voluptuous Daphne. He was never going to leave her as his life was too good right now.

He'd liked to call to Daphne across the shop by his nickname for her DeeDee, no one ever suspected the real meaning behind it, she would laugh and they would wobble.

Frieda was o.k. for a bit of fun
but DeeDee was the only real match for his appetite, God he missed that 'gal'.
(Everybody did!)

Lee's Face book page was like a 'who's who list' of local yummy mummies but his wife understood that there 'was no harm in it babe'. He mostly referred to all his lady-friends generically as it saved slip-ups and complications.

'All right darling, how's it going' he'd ooze down the phone regularly...'when shall I come over and trim your bush for ya?' his raw, boyish humour and over confidence were definitely part of his charm. He laughed in a deep and throaty way as if he'd spent the morning chewing stinging nettles, then took his Nike cap off momentarily to let the steam out and shifted himself about in his fake, loose, Louis Vuitton jeans.

GILBERT

Gilbert, the salon's most recent member to the management team, had been selected for his extensive experience in the hairdressing trade. All salons benefited from having mature staff on their shop floor, as they brought a settling

atmosphere. Hairdresser's could easily get over-run with young trainees, which although gave a business vibrancy and street-cred, could also get a little too boisterous and if you weren't careful as the owner, Barbara, knew only too well, could quickly turn into something that resembled a night-club with loud music and offensive language.

The 'Yin and Yang' of the energies as Gilbert had stated at his interview. 'Babs' had liked his analogy and once he had continued on to explain that he could improve on the shop's feng shui and that this would unquestionably lead to new-found luck and prosperity, his new job was 'in the bag,' so to speak.

He mystically suggested that she place 2 lively goldfish, near the entrance, swimming in a large bowl to encourage wealthier customers and, for her, to make doubly-sure that she regularly closed all the loo seats (so as not to flush her good fortune away).

Also to twirl a pirouette every-time she entered her business... (This last suggestion, he'd added from his 'own book of well-being' and was just for his own amusement.) He smiled confidently and momentarily held her hand, palm-up, as if he could watch her world unfolding in it and then he chuckled knowingly, leading Barbara to believe that all was well...and Gilbert could indeed 'see,' that it mostly was.

As he had lent in towards her, however, he had smelt the sickly scent of last night's perfume, heavy drinking and cigar-smoke about her. He stared deeply into her tired, trusting, dried-up and smudged mascaraed eyes and easily slipped into his alter ego. His shoulders slumped momentarily, as he was apparently, 'taken over by spirit' and quite incredibly foretold her that...

'You like to party, like a bit of a drink, don't you Barbara. I can see that you've been hurt in the past... and you have a totem animal with you, a white spirit cat, no wait, I'm wrong there...he's not crossed over, he lives with you, this feline lives with you, doesn't he? You're HIS person aren't you'... which Gilbert was correct about, as her beloved, Tomsk, had left a telling trail of shed fur upon her lap just that morning...'and I'm being told that it's probably time you went for an eye test...have you noticed that your sight hasn't been so good lately?' he expanded, in a trance-like state, waving his free hand about convincingly, having seen the remainders of her eggy breakfast that had dripped down onto her blouse earlier that she had failed to notice and her all-revealing, unkempt eyebrows….(if she could of seen the bushy-slugs creeping across her fore-head, surely she would of plucked the dreadful things into shape by now, he assumed, especially being in the beauty trade and all! Pah!)

(No shit, Sherlock!)

It was a shame that Gilbert would often lie and show-boat like this, as he was naturally, very perceptive, but it was just so damn easy for him to read people in this way. He fabricated to folk, if they asked, that he was very proud and grateful of his Romany-roots. Then, he would often confide in a hushed and secretive tone as an after-thought, that it would be incredibly fortuitous for them, if they were to 'gift' some paper-money his way, but they shouldn't feel obliged to. Nor would it hurt, if they then proceeded to buy themselves a scratch-card or two from the lovely lady at the local Co-Op store and if they were to have a big win, not to forget him, nudge-nudge, ha ha.

He would then clap and blow three times, purely for theatrical effect. However, he did believe, that one day, whilst doing this silly ritual, that he might accidently, fart instead and actually disappear into thin air or indeed leave this world, up his own arse.

Phhhhhfffttttttt.....alakazam.....poof

                    CURTAIN CALL!!!!!

Gilbert arrived early to work. He liked to, particularly on a Thursday as Wednesday was a very good day for tips, it was the day they did special offers and customers loved that and became very generous towards the stylists.

He opened the front door, using a clean tissue to hold the handle and eased the door, back with his foot, then quickly turned about and locked the door from the inside. Still holding the tissue, he switched the light on, then off, then on, then off, then finally on, at the count of 3 and left the switch alone.

He hung up his scarf but not his jacket, grabbed a clean cloth that he'd bleached over-night and began to check around the salon for wayward strands of hair wound around the sinks and any residual 'scuuum'. Which also gave him the opportunity to slip a few coins from each of the other senior staff's 'tip' boxes into his own pocket. Lee's being his most favourite to target. Gil would never steal from the junior staff, as he felt that they didn't earn enough for a McDonald's burger, let alone a half decent meal...poor things, 'I've been there too many times myself' he would reflect.

He tapped his watch, thinking...yes, there was just enough time. He walked to the reception desk, opened the till and helped himself to an extra couple of pound coins...no one ever noticed the missing cash, as long as you weren't greedy. Satisfied at last, he unlocked the door and the work-force began arriving almost immediately.

In the staff room, Gilbert remarked that they were out of coffee and as it was such a handsome day outside, that he would go and buy some and at the same time, he felt like treating everyone to cakes. He had a strange set of morals and codes of conduct. He did believe that you should 'give back' occasionally. He left the salon, blinked for a moment in the sunshine, turned left and headed straight for the bookies.

'I'd like 'A Quick Leg Over' at Cheltenham today please,' he said in one breath, '£10 to win,' he added with a harmless, glint in his eye. He did so love a little early morning windfall, if he were a dog; he'd be wagging his tail in circles. The cashier bristled and sat-up stiffly in her chair, she didn't much care for his lewd innuendo...she had to put up with this type of crap all day long from punters and for the minimum wage as well...'sniff,' her mother had always said that she should have trained for banking but she'd gone and got herself 'banged-up' with a baby at 17...something that her mum would never let her forget...and now look at her stuck in this dump...look at him! Bloody, making indecent remarks towards her...'dirty, old man,' she thought.

'Have a good day,' Gilbert said benignly, picking up his gambling slip 'I'll be back for my winnings later!'

'Good day,' she retorted, robotically, her voice completely devoid of any warmth. 'Oh sod right off,' she was thinking, 'filthy perv', letching over me,' and began tugging at her black, polo-neck sweater, upwards by its long neck, in case he could see any of her bare flesh.

He wasn't looking of course, why, he'd worked amongst beautiful woman his whole life and this particular lady, he didn't find attractive in any way. To be totally honest, she looked about as cheerful as a traffic-warden chewing on a wasp sandwich. He felt that it was his duty to try and 'jolly her along a bit, poor, wee soul,' he felt sorry for her...life can't be easy when you look that awful and her buck teeth, hell, did her boyfriend feed her on carrots and pony-nuts? Gil was now, silently, contemplating their sex life, too bloody risky he concluded, one misplaced sneeze and his wedding-tackle could be munched off... I bet he doesn't like to upset her before going to the boudoir! He was really amusing himself now but somehow managed to keep his face in neutral-gear and not laugh.

However, he did enjoy making people feel good about themselves, it was part of his job, and so departed with a bullshit compliment about her smile, (which he most definitely had not witnessed) saying that it could light a room up, and gave her a playful wink. Maybe he'd buy her a fresh cream cake too and make her day...

The woman turned away from him, repulsed. She made eye contact with another young member of staff and playfully stuck her fingers into her mouth and pretended to make herself sick....'bluarghhhh.'

#classy

ELVIS

It's a long and unlikely story how Arthur came to be in the 'Pork Pie and Whippet' pub this night and so I shall save that story for another time. But rest assured, he was there and much to his delight it turned out to be a lively evening of Elvis Presley impersonators and burlesque dancers.. Takings had been a bit low lately. Dave, the landlord, recently had to find cash to replace the green felt on his pool tables and 'God knows where all the cue chalk went, did they eat the bloody stuff? Not, to mention the rolls and rolls of loo paper they got through weekly. Quite frankly, it was as busy as the public toilet in Liverpool St Station, not that he made a point of hanging out in the men's conveniences, you understand.....well not too often, but there was that time a couple of years ago....

(I'll tell you about that too, another day.)

'Are you lonesome tonight,' Elvis was singing when Arthur arrived at the busy pub, 'too right I am' he thought, Daphne had been gone some time now and he was missing a woman's touch. He bought his drink and settled himself away from the bar but near the stage, 'thank God for some 'life' at last' he thought to himself. Elvis continued with, 'You were always on my mind' and Arthur's spirit sank as he began to wonder if it hadn't been such a good idea to come here after all... Thankfully, the impersonator finished and was painfully, slow clapped off.

Gilbert, Daphne's replacement at the salon, was sat across from the window with his sterile hand-wipes out cleaning the table top and sipping his G&T slowly. He was glad to be sitting down as it had been a very hard day on his feet with back-to-back clients.

Soon after, intriguingly, a huge teapot the size of a mini was dragged out center stage, in front of the curious crowd and then there was a 10 minute break to give the punters time to buy another pint.

Suddenly, the compare grabbed the microphone 'Bon Jovi' style and shouted across the noisy room,

'Please put your hands together for the one and only, the gorgeous, irrepressible........ Deeeee....licious Deloris!!

Right on her cue, Deloris, who had been crouched inside the teapot waiting patiently and was now fighting off cramp in her big toe, jumped up with the lid firmly attached to her head and her large pendulous breasts aswinging with just a couple of fake slices of Battenburg cake stuck about her body precariously, to preserve her modesty!

'I'm a little tea-pot, short and stout,' she started to sing in a very low and husky voice. The pub went mad for her, whistling and cheering her on... the burlesque dancer continued to sing, as she did her best to climb from the pot in a sexy fashion, which if you've ever tried to do such a thing in a gee-string and high-heels, you will know just how tricky this can be. She held out her hand toward Arthur, trying to steady herself, Arthur jumped gallantly to her side, whereby the pot toppled over and Deloris ended up falling painfully onto Arthur, squashing his face with her knockers, causing Arthur to have an Asama attack from pure excitement....... Arthur believed he was going to die in that exquisite moment, but did later reminisce on the evening's events, that there were much worse ways 'to go'...

As you can imagine this event made quite an impact on Arthur and quite frankly he felt he would certainly endure another Asama attack to feel that Divine creature on top of him once more.

There was another short break and then the evening's entertainment continued and was a great success.

Gil finally gave into the sensation that he needed to head to the 'the little boy's room,' before leaving the pub for home and duly headed that way. A quick clean-up around the cubicle with his wet-wipes before relieving himself and then he took 2 cardboard inner-tubes from his inside pocket, balanced them on the back of the loo and replaced back into his jacket, 2 full rolls of toilet paper. Smugly, he thought to himself that...,'exchange is no robbery' and on passing Dave by the bar, as he went to leave, casually remarked over his shoulder that,

'The loo's are out of paper again, it really isn't good enough,...I could always take my custom along the road to the 'Pheasant Pluckers Arms,' if you don't start to look after your customers any better.'

'Goodnight Gil,' Dave called after him quite fondly but quietly added to himself, 'and good riddance'.

The next morning, Arthur sent an impressive bouquet of flowers to Deloris's office, requesting the pleasure of her company for dinner.....

Deloris arrived home exhausted and bruised after falling from the giant tea-pot (she was quite possibly the only woman to ever have sustained such an injury). She poured herself a night-cap and sank into a rather sumptuous settee, it was a blissful moment. She eased her stilettos off which had blistered her heels and in an instant had removed her bra from underneath her home-knitted, wooly sweater. The under wires had been digging into her voluptuous body, that of which, was surely moulded upon the soft, rolling welsh hills and valleys.

Her lounge had silk scarves draped around lamp shades and luxurious throws casually lain about the chairs and a small chandelier with purple, multi-faceted droplets sending dancing light around the walls. A wood-burner crackled welcomingly in the corner and her small dog, Alan, sat comfortably on her lap...he was never happier. Whilst away in a quiet corner, coiled around a piece of tree-stump, rested a large snake which she periodically danced, professionally with. Deloris, finished her brandy, rested her head backwards on the couch and within an instant was snoring as loudly as a bull-frog on a mating night..

The following morning she went to her office which she shared with a group of local entertainers, they manned it between them on a daily rotation. They answered the phone and took bookings. This actually worked out quite well for most of the time, although occasionally there were discrepancies over the fairness of job allocations. There were comedians, singers other burlesque and specialty acts based there.....their office outings and parties were always loud and outrageous.

Deloris was surprised and delighted on receiving her bouquet from Arthur but after a short time of deliberation decided that on balance, it would probably not be a good idea to meet up with him again, although she had enjoyed his attention and sparkly blue eyes the previous evening. She did, however, have the good manners to call and explain her decision to the disappointed Arthur but couldn't help herself expanding on the truth and so declared that she was soon to be taking up an amazing job-offer in Las Vegas which was something she'd always wanted to do.

Apparently, the Americans would just love her English accent over there and her unusual acts.

Meanwhile, at the salon, Gilbert had a brilliant idea of beginning a Christmas-box club which all the staff could use to save some money until nearer the date. He suggested that they draw their cash back out from it, at the beginning of December and that he would record all payments in his notebook for future reference. The staff could save in £5, £10 or £20 increments weekly, whichever was a comfortable amount for them. The staff collectively agreed that Christmas was a very expensive time of the year and that Gil's saving club was a good idea and obediently went to raid their tip-boxes and then waited patiently whilst Gil began to record each amount, scribbling quickly with his small pencil. Receipts could be collected later if they wished but he was too busy to issue them now as he had a client under the dryer, waiting for him to return before her hair spontaneously combusted.

Gil felt such a sense of self-satisfaction at the positive response to his idea, that during his lunch-time break scurried along to the Virgin holiday shop in the High St and chose a brochure to day-dream from, an early winter vacation to Vancouver would be very nice indeed... Afterwards, he went to place a generous bet on 'Food Poisoning' to win at Aintree.

Arthur felt crestfallen after his call from Deloris but being the ever tenacious man that he was, begun to scour the local paper for more local events, such as........burlesque dancing.....he really had to see that luscious, song-bird once more before she left for the bright lights of America.

SARAH

Frieda was feeling rather neglected by Lee who was too busy flirting with his pretty, young customer Sarah to notice. She was here to have her highlights re-done. Frieda shot a filthy look at them both laughing away together and as soon as Lee caught her looking their way, he called across,

'Hey Frieda, could you mix-up Sarah's hair colour for me, thanks darling' and winked at her. She skulked away to do as she'd been asked but thought it might be '*nice*' if Sarah's high-lights were a bit brighter than usual and decided to add double the peroxide to the paste....'that should do nicely' she thought coldly, and then delivered it across the salon to Lee who was now rubbing his client's shoulders because she had a bad knot 'just there.'

Lee continued to work his way across Sarah's head applying the blond highlight mixture as he went and wrapping each section in silver-foil. Once he'd finished, he asked if she would like a coffee to which she replied yes and Lee once again called across to Frieda to,

'Make Sarah a coffee would you? Black, no sugar...I'm just going to pop-out for a quick sandwich.'

Frieda made her coffee, black **with** sugar, intentionally, and left it by Sarah's chair, spilling a little as she did, just enough to leave some liquid in the saucer, ready to drip off from the bottom of the cup, once it was lifted.

After his lunch, Lee began to remove the foils from Sarah's head. The hair was rather white but worse still, as he continued, pieces of her hair were breaking off which he desperately tried to conceal in the palm of his hand, 'Oh God, no,' he felt sick inside and once all the foils had been removed he quietly took Sarah to the sink to wash the peroxide away. It was awful, the sink was covered in her hair but thankfully she couldn't see that, as he had quickly swapped a flannel to cover her eyes during washing, to a towel to dry her face with and swiftly turned her chair away from the evidence. The blood had drained from Lee's face, he just didn't know what the hell to do next.

As that moment, an unlikely saviour walked past in the form of Gilbert, he gave Lee a look of utter despair as he took in the catastrophe before him but within a moment, gathered himself together and remarked breezily to Sarah that such a pretty girl, really shouldn't hide her lovely face under all that hair and why didn't she let Lee give her a complete make-over and go for a sexy-short nymph style to compliment her petite features and if she had the time, the beautician would give her a free whole new look too, so that they could take a few utterly gorgeous advertising photos of her for their web-page. Sarah was so flattered by all the attention that she readily agreed to his plan, totally unaware of the car-crash that had happened to her....

At the end of the day Lee shook Gil's hand firmly and genuinely thanked him for getting him out of his scrape and then left to secretly meet Frieda in the car-park.

'Ain't nothing for you to worry about babe, that Sarah's just a bit obsessed about me, that's all, I'd get rid of her if I could but she's a good customer ain't she?' he said as he pulled the young woman closer to himself and began to kiss her passionately.

'Why don't we go somewhere a bit quieter,' she suggested but Lee continued to hold her tightly as he explained that he would love that but had to get back home to his wife as she was 'being a right cow lately' during these last few weeks of her pregnancy...

'I mustn't be late,' he said going to check his watch, but it was missing and he presumed he must have left it by the sink at work although he had no recollection of doing so......

Beneath her coat, he ran his hands across her beautiful, slim body, twanged her bra-strap to lighten the mood and within two minutes had left her standing there alone, whilst he drove off in his scruffy, old BMW. She kept thinking over and over, that Lee had said he would like to 'get rid of Sarah', get rid, get rid. The intrusive thought just would not stop.

Frieda felt so unhappy that tears welled up in her eyes and she looked around for something to distract herself with. Consequently, she headed off to the take-away pizzeria, where she was greeted warmly by the three brothers that worked there together. Anthony paid particular attention to her and asked,

'Ehi, come sei bella?' ... Frieda looked up into his deep brown eyes and her heart smiled once again.

Gilbert, meanwhile, was in the 'Pheasant Pluckers Arms' public house, having a large G&T, whilst looking for a likely candidate to sell a cracking little watch to...

LYNDSAY

'Bye gorgeous, see you tomorrow after work, don't have our baby without me...,' Lee laughed at his own pathetic wit

'Have a good day,' she said, 'see you tomorrow bae,' Lee rubbed her belly gently,

'Don't give your Mum a hard time today, ya hear me in there!.' he said and kissed her tenderly. Lyndsay sighed tiredly and told him not to be silly and assured him that she would be fine by herself.

He had previously lied to his wife, that he was having a night out with the boys straight after work that evening and would be sleeping-over at his mates house, it was Saturday after all and he deserved a night out once in a while didn't he 'babe,' to which she had wearily agreed. There really was no point in disagreeing with him as he always did exactly what he wanted to regardless of her feelings.

There was another busy day at the salon, Lee was always in demand and the customers seemed to love him. As the day was drawing to a close, he had inadvertently left his phone in the staff-room and Gilbert, ever the light-fingered, opportunist, had swiftly pocketed it with the intention of selling it on. Gil had quite a gambling habit to support and unfortunately, he wasn't on a winning streak right now but like he always said, 'The sun will come out tomorrow!' but no one was ever quite sure what he meant by that, as it often rained the next day???

Lee was so excited about his forth-coming night with Sarah that as soon as he had collected his wage slip and gave Gilbert £10 towards the Christmas saving club that all the staff contributed to, he left work immediately. Frieda soon ran after him, catching him up as he was about to leave the car-park.

'Hey,' she shouted waving her arms frantically, 'where are you off to in such a hurry?' her jealous streak alive and glowing in her mad, green eyes.

'Hey princess,' Lee replied calmly and softly through his open car window, 'I got to get home to look after Jordon (his young son), Lyndsay's going out tonight,' he lied convincingly and then grabbed Frieda by her coat collar and kissed her roughly, pushing his tongue deep into her mouth (he mistakenly thought that she enjoyed it that way).

'Look, we'll get some time together soon, maybe next week, ...hey, don't look at me like that, there's nothing I can do about it, Lyndsay's a selfish bitch, you know?' he said looking injured, 'come 'ere,' and again nearly choked her with his frenzied kisses and pressed his hands firmly against her young skin. She pulled away, she really didn't like it when he touched her like this, it was the same as when he'd had a few too many drinks...he got heavy handed.

'I'll see you Monday!' and immediately sped off.

Frieda stood a little bewildered for a few moments. Once again her mind was racing with negative thoughts.....'that bastard, how dare he treat me like that' but then a moment later, already counter balancing them with softer, sexier and more devious plans of an unexpected visit to his home, maybe that very evening for a surprise seduction whilst his wife was away. She could put on her new lingerie that he had chosen for her during their lunch-break. She had paid for it though, as he only had his credit card on him and his 'Mrs' always checked his statements thoroughly, he explained.

'Sorry darling, I'll pay you back,' he enthused but never did, 'you'll look amazing in them pink panties, hon,' he said, taking a moment to imagine her in them.

****
****
****

Lee hurried around to Sarah's house as horny as a bull, in a field full of Friesians, carrying a gift-bag of almost identical satin under ware, only these were in purple and a slightly larger size.

At 7pm, Lee's phone begun ringing inside Gilbert's coat and then a text arrived, simply saying,

'Lee come home I think the baby's coming.' Gil, who was in the bookies, sat rooted to the spot...the message, was from Lyndsay, Lee's wife,

'Think, think, think, what to do, what to do?....' Gil panicked and frantically started pulling out wet-wipes to clean the fruit-machine he was sitting in front of.....

15 minutes later there was another message and then another and another......

Gilbert remained stunned and blindly continued to watch for the 3 lucky 7's to light up the slot machine but... they never did. Just like babies really, you never quite knew when to expect them.

RONNY

This evening, Arthur was going to the pub hopefully to see the gorgeous Deloris perform again.

He'd recently been watching 'The Morning Show' and had been given some very useful information on the latest men's grooming techniques. The last time he'd gone out of his way to impress a woman, he'd splashed a little Old Spice aftershave about his body a bit and removed some hard skin from his feet. Now it seemed that a woman's expectations had increased rather a lot. He must now be perfectly moisturised and any spare hair must be gone!

I would like to point out at this juncture that I do not agree with this line of torture and I believe it to be barbaric along with other such-like craziness as injecting poison into your lips for the much sought after 'trout pout'…..'go figure' that???? Personally, I would prefer to look like a Halibut (and some would rightly say that I already do :).

Anyway, Arthur had made an appointment at 'The Curl Up n Dye' beauty salon, A place he felt comfortable with as Daphne his wife, had worked there for years before she had left them both. A couple of the staff still recognised him and on arrival, Rita greeted him warmly, with a big smile and asked

'You're first time here for a treatment with us Arthur?'…..'back, crack and sac is it?' She was having trouble not to giggle at his naivety.

'So,' she continued, 'if you'd just like to make your way into cubicle 2, take all your clothes off, cover up with this (tiny) towel if you wish, (gave him a small plastic cup and some Play Boy magazines….O.K. so I lied about that bit :) and Ronny will be with you shortly.

Thankfully, Ronny turned out to be a strapping 6-foot man with tattoos and piercings and not a pretty, young thing as he had feared.

Ronny, begun by waxing his back, that Arthur found surprisingly uncomfortable but bearable. Ronny was holding onto a strong desire to joke that 'it would have been easier to strip a Silver Back gorilla'....such a hairy man! But his professionalism prevented him from saying so.

Next crack....

'O.K. take a deep breath for me,' Ronny said and added 'did you see the rugby match at the weekend?' He was doing his best to keep his client calm and then 'ccccrrrrrippp,' off came the wax in an 'out of body, leaving experience'. Albert's bum cheeks were singed from the brutality of the act and lastly....le sac

'You're doing really well,' Ronny tried to assure him 'but this can be a little tender around here,' and slathered his private parts in burning, hot wax. The beautician was fully aware of the impending pain he was about to inflict upon the man and he began to perspire heavily….'got to detach myself from the situation,' he thought, as all beauticians have to, from time to time. Arthur too was desperately trying to keep himself composed when suddenly off came the wax with such speed and aggression that he almost hit the roof with the shock, he was writhing about in agony,

'Shut the front door,' he hollered out in pain, (not exactly what he said but you get the gist). He'd just paid £50 for this huge brute of a man to abuse him. His left testicle immediately swelled to the size of a tennis ball, fiery red from the vicious onslaught. Ronny quickly slapped on some cooling aloe-vera, wiped his own moist brow and with a mischievous grin, quietly said,

'And now the other side, Sir.'

But Arthur was having none of it, he'd leaped from the table and was hopping from foot to foot, splashing water on his manhood by the small sink in the corner of the room, convinced that part of his 'family jewels' had just been torn from his body. Had he carried on dancing much longer, Ronny believed that he would surely have brought on rain.

Later that evening, Arthur reflected on examining himself 'down there,' that he really couldn't make out any improvement and didn't understand why any woman would be attracted to 'his purple, knap sack' looking like a plucked, half starved, strung-up turkey.....

gobble gobble

NELSON

Frieda's image of herself as a steamy mistress, turning up unexpectedly at Lee's house with only her pink under-ware and high heels on discreetly hidden beneath her rain-coat very much appealed to her. She believed that his wife was out for the evening and although she knew it was risky, the adrenalin that cascaded throughout her made the plan irresistible. She quickly showered and was now, certainly, in the mood for some fun.

Frieda wanted to spend as much time this evening with him as possible and knew that Jordon, his young son, would usually be in bed by 7.30. It was just another of her reckless acts that she regularly felt compelled to do. Excitedly, she made her way from the bus stop towards Lee's home with her heart racing

Meanwhile, Gilbert's conscience finally got the better of him and he had begun an attempt to locate Lee. (Gil, would lie that he had found Lee's phone by the outside door of the salon and not stolen it as was the real case….he would be the hero and not the villain just for once and he quite liked how that felt). Gil began to text around some of the staff to see if any of them knew of his whereabouts.

Lyndsay, Lee's wife, had phoned for an ambulance because of the excruciating pain of her contractions. She had tried in vain to contact her husband and had assured herself that he must be in a noisy pub for him not to have heard her desperate calls.

****
****

Unbeknown to her, Lee was already 'taking' Sarah for the second time that evening. The first time had been across the top of her marble-laminate, kitchen units whilst the 'ships-cat' watched from his dirt-tray, taking a crap, and for the second time he'd pinned her to the front-door, deftly tied her hands to the inside of the letter-box with her bra and gagged her with her new knickers. His role-play could be quite extreme at times.

Sometimes, he wouldn't hear from a girlfriend again, after a 'first night', as not all of his lady friends were quite comfortable with his unexpected sex games but he 'really didn't give a damn whether he did or not. There was rarely a woman that he really cared for (Daphne, having been the most recent one to have almost captured his heart).

He left Sarah, naked and attached to the door,

'Stay there ma'am.. I'll be back in a mo,' he said, tickling her with a feather duster and bowing deeply, being true to his assumed character. He then went to check his phone for texts, but to his extreme annoyance found that his mobile was missing, where upon Nelson's flagpole was immediately lowered and Lady Hamilton was untied and released from the crow's nest, temporarily, to eat their lasagna, both still naked and then catch up on the latest episode of 'Coronation Street' before adult fun resumed at the arrival of some animated meerkats. (Which reminds me that, I must renew my car insurance!)

Frieda arrived at Lee's home just in time to see his heavily pregnant wife being assisted into an ambulance and a neighbour, consoling her little boy, promising him that 'Mummy would be o.k.'

'I want my Daddy,' Jordon was crying out but his Father was once again, busily 'sinking a large boat' and tracing a fast-melting, strawberry Cornetto around the contours of Emma Hamilton's body.

It had been a close run between frolicking with an ice cream or playing hoopla around his 'THANG,' with a bag of large, frozen, calamari rings.....but really, which one would you have opted for??? :b

'Where the hell was Lee?' Frieda was turning the question over in her mind as she watched the ambulance leave his house for the hospital with his expectant wife, Lyndsay, on board. Her stomach lurched as the realization quickly came to her suspicious mind, that he was surely with another woman and it was Sarah that she immediately thought of. She knew where Sarah lived, as she had already stalked her a couple of times in a jealous rage, watching to see if Lee would visit in his beaten up BMW. Which to her relief, he hadn't on those occasions.

However, that son of a bitch was probably cheating on her and his wife after all! She began running back to the bus stop furiously. She was going around to Sarah's now to confront her and if that bastard was there, she would tell his wife everything...'never mind the new baby' she cruelly thought.

Before she visited her enemy she charged home, changed into her black Lycra gym kit, tied her hair up and shoved a sports cap low on her head to hide her fierce eyes and roughly pushed a baseball bat (that she kept for protection, by her bed) and a towel into her old college backpack, which still carried her over-stuffed pencil case and beloved tatty diary, before setting off…..'I'm gonna teach that son of a bitch a lesson that he'll never forget,' she thought.

On arriving at Sarah's, Frieda spotted Lee's car discreetly parked around the corner in a quiet spot which was convenient for her, as she then set about smashing his windscreen and headlights with her bat, which did relieve a little of her tension but not enough to stop her in her tracks. She turned away, picking broken glass fragments from her clothing and slowly walked towards the house swallowing down the bile and hatred that had risen into her mouth.

She peered in the front window but could see nothing through the net curtains, however she could hear the television was on. The crazed woman crept around the side of the house and silently tried the back door which opened beneath her fingertips, she stepped inside...

****

Frieda stepped into a dishevelled kitchen, the crime scene had all of
the recognisable trappings of some 'fun time' with Lee. There was squashed food about and plates and dishes that had been hastily removed from the work surfaces, in the height of their passion, had been piled carelessly on the floor, one of which was broken, that she stepped carefully across heading towards the hallway.

The shower was running but all she could hear was her own heavy, excited breath. This time, right now, she was going to 'catch him'. There had been so many times when she had thought that he was lying and cheating on her...she reached around for her bat and, oh so quietly, slipped up-stairs.

The bedroom door was ajar and when she glanced in she could see that Sarah was tied somewhat uncomfortably to the bed, gagged and blindfolded. She looked cold and vulnerable, lying hopelessly naked, which had an unexpected calming effect on Frieda. Her enragement immediately softened and was replaced with empathy for the young woman. She now understood that Sarah was just another victim of Lee's predatory personality and self-indulgence. Frieda placed the bat and back-pack, quietly against the wall. Lee was taking his time, as was his usual way, in the bathroom. She walked towards the bed, her eyes totally transfixed on Sarah's beautiful olive skin, so different to her own freckles. Gently, she took off the handkerchief that was around her mouth and put a finger to the woman's lips for her to stay quiet. She touched her inquisitively and delicately traced the dragon tattoo that ran along the side of her body with her forefinger. Frieda's skin began to tingle, (how different to the way he had been touching her earlier, she thought unknowingly) both women were enjoying the moment.

The shower was turned off and the spell between the ladies was broken, as Frieda's temper returned, flooding her with adrenaline. Suddenly, she was very aware that she had to leave but not before writing a chilling message for that cheating bastard. She quickly reached into her bag, grabbed her pencil case, took a black marker pen out and boldly wrote across Sarah's stomach, taking great care not to startle her. She then untied Sarah's legs and lastly one arm so that she could now free herself and Frieda ran for her life out of there, carelessly grabbing her bat and bag as she left, leaving Sarah still blindfolded.

As Sarah took the scarf off from her eyes, Lee was standing in the doorway, fully dressed. The marker pen was on the floor, between them.

'What the hell's going on?' he exclaimed, seeing that she was, for the most part, now untied from the bed.

'You were leaving?' she asked simultaneously. Both were confused…'what the fuck? You've written on me?' she said, looking down at herself.

'You crazy bitch, what is this?' all pleasantries were quickly disappearing, neither one of them understood the real situation...yet. Lee stepped forward and read the message that had been written across the woman's body, it simply read...

BYE BYE BABY

'You wrote that and was gonna leave, just like that, what kind of a creep are you Lee?'

Lee's mind went into overdrive, what was she going on about, obviously he hadn't written it, he'd been in the bathroom,

'You didn't write this?' he asked cautiously helping Sarah to free her last hand

'No, of course, I didn't write it, you left me fucking tied up you piece of shit,'

'Then how did you get free?...' his voice trailed off, he didn't like the look of this one bit, he just wanted to get away from her...maybe her boyfriend had turned up unexpectedly 'look I've got to go, I've lost my phone and I don't know what the hell's going on here, I'll call you...o.k?' He was already exiting the bedroom,

'You mother-fucker!' she yelled, 'get out, get out!' and slung a trainer at his retreating head.

....
....

'Fuuuuck,' Lee shouted on discovering that his car had been smashed-up. His brain couldn't take it all in, he furtively looked around him, certain that he was about to get attacked by Sarah's jealous partner. He fumbled, taking the keys from his pocket as his hands were shaking so badly, brushed aside some of the fallen glass and within moments was driving away.

Having left the immediate area, Lee began to concoct a set of lies to cover his tracks, to explain to his wife how his phone had got stolen and his car had got 'done-over' whilst parked outside the pub, but on arriving home, he soon discovered a note on the table, from Lyndsay, telling him that their baby was on the way.

On arriving at the hospital, Lee ran to find his wife, over-come with guilt. He found her in a side room. He looked in, and in that instant regretted every other woman he'd ever slept with, she was just so unbelievable serene and angelic, sitting there in the shafts of pink, early morning light. She'd turned a blind eye to his extra-marital affairs so many times.

Unfortunately for him, he had missed the birth as the baby had been delivered very quickly and already Lyndsay was peacefully, nursing her. He stepped in sheepishly,

'I'm so sorry, sweet-heart,' he began, and gently held them both in a treasured moment. Lee's eye's filled with tears, he was full of regret and, in that soul searching second, made a vow to himself, that he would never cheat on the Mother of his children, ever again, 'my phones been stolen…,' he stuttered out,

'Not now,' she quietly interrupted her husband, trying to sooth him 'shh,' she could hardly bring herself to look at him, the hurt ran so painfully within her, she still loved him so deeply, 'I'm sorry too,' she murmured and gently took the baby away from her breast, for Lee to see her for the first time, and as he looked down upon the beautiful little girl, he knew immediately that…she was not his.

DELORIS

Arthur arrived at the 'Aching Elbow', public house. He was almost certain that his girl, Deloris, would be performing there that evening. The advert in the local paper had read, 'Burlesque and Belly Dancing, Tonight!' He'd had to wait 3 weeks before tracking her down to here.

He took his drink and sat by the small, cleared area at the end of the pub and waited hopefully.

Presently, Deloris did arrive on the impromptu 'stage', rolling her tummy and shimmying backward. She had an enormous, lacquered and back-combed hair-do, in the 60's it would have been referred to as a bee-hive, that seemed to have a life all of its own and gaily bounced about independently. Her arms were elegantly extended out to her sides, whilst a very large, brightly coloured, parrot hopped about over her shoulders and occasionally swayed a bit from side to side (presumably, dancing to the music, lol). Deloris past Brazil nuts up to him, from a crystal-encrusted bag, that she had jiggling about on her bronzed, fatty hips...Arthur was entranced and shuffled about on his seat in excitement.

Deloris glided across to a large, upright, wicker, laundry basket that had been dragged to the corner of the 'show-area'. She took a small, penny whistle out, that she'd had tucked away inside her exotically, tasselled bra, and began to play a short, Egyptian melody. The lid slipped off the basket and a mighty python lifted his head from inside. The crowd moved their seats, uneasily, a little further away, and one or two of them actually left the area all together...The heat was on. She grappled with the almighty snake, to lift it from its resting place, and as she struggled to get him onto her shoulders, the excited macaw flew across the mesmerised crowd, flying towards the open fire-exit. They'd never seen such a spectacle on a damp, Tuesday night.

'Someone shut the bloody door!' Deloris shouted out across the din, staggering under the sheer weight of the reptile about her neck, 'quick!' she yelled out. Thankfully, the entrance was banged shut, just ahead of the enormous bird which seemed to upset him immensely, and he swiftly turned, squawking loudly and flew low, across the audience, buzzing some heads with his immense blue wings, as he passed in a very unsettling way. The crowd shrieked, some in fear and some in delight. One man dropped his glasses and another spat his false teeth out, and they chattered to the floor, amongst the ensuing melee. The parrot dive-bombed the bar, causing absolute carnage and then it finally returned to Deloris, whereby he landed on her head momentarily, screeching and bopping about like he was squashing grapes and in an instant flew off once again with her hair attached to his crusty, yellow talons. Deloris shrieked and buckled to the floor, sobbing, and the snake slid quietly away into the terrorised onlookers, who immediately parted like the Red Sea.

Arthur was already up from his chair and by her side, comforting her,

'My snake,' she whispered, with a trembling voice, 'please find him for me,' she looked into Arthur's face with huge tears in her liquid, topaz eyes and he was immediately stirred into action. He grabbed his large overcoat and headed towards the shouting men and hysterical woman that were clambering across tables and chairs.

'Get back!' Arthur bellowed with great authority, and threw his coat across the snakes head and held him firmly until Deloris joined him. Together they carried the huge beast back to his basket, where he quickly settled down to devour a frozen mouse that Deloris had brought along for him, as a little treat for her 'Big boy...'

The macaw, however, was going to be much trickier to catch, as he had settled high amongst the old beams that run across the ceiling, and now he seemed to be either mating or nesting with Deloris's wig.

'We'll not get him down from there,' Deloris said, 'not until he's ready to, come on let's have a drink...what did you say your name was again?'

'Arthur,' he replied, 'I sent you some flowers a while back, do you remember?'

'Yes,' she exclaimed, 'of course, now I do and they were so beautiful too, thank you so much, you're my hero, Arthur, my hero,' and as she stood before him with her own hair, crazily looking like she'd jumped in the bath with her hairdryer, and skimpy, bejewelled knickers, Arthur slid his coat, protectively,

around her meaty shoulders and Deloris gave
him a big wet kiss and cuddled him against
her heaving bosoms. ☺

A Happy Ending x

Confessions

Of

A

Hairdresser

Samphire Bobobang

All characters in this book are fictional except the ones that aren't ☺.

For 'The Best Mum In The World'

&

My amazing lads, Max & Alfie

(I love you all, so much.)

xxx

Printed in Great Britain
by Amazon